D0594335

SPROUT AND THE DOGSITTER

Books by Jenifer Wayne

Sprout
Sprout's Window Cleaner
Sprout and the Helicopter

SPROUT AND THE DOGSITTER

Jenifer Wayne

Illustrated by Gail Owens

McGraw-Hill Book Company
New York   St. Louis   San Francisco

First published and distributed in the United States of America
by McGraw-Hill Inc., 1977. All Rights Reserved.
Printed in the United States of America.

1 2 3 4 5 M U B P 7 8 9 8 7

Library of Congress Cataloging in Publication Data

Wayne, Jenifer.
  Sprout and the dogsitter.

  SUMMARY: Sprout joins a party of carol singers on
Christmas Eve but before the evening is over loses both
them and his new coat.
  [1. Christmas stories] I. Owens, Gail.   II. Ti-
title.
PZ7.W35128Sod   [Fic]   76-56109
ISBN 0-07-068696-3 lib. bdg.

SPROUT AND THE DOGSITTER

1

Sprout was eating his fourth piece of toast.

"What a lot," said Tilly. She sat on her stool and cushion opposite him at the kitchen table and looked at him with round-eyed admiration. "How does he eat such a lot?" she asked.

"He's a big boy," said their mother, "and he's hungry when he comes home from school."

Sprout finished the toast and took a piece of Swiss cheese.

"I want to be a big boy and go to school," said Tilly.

"Don't be silly," said Sprout with his mouth full. "You're a girl."

For a moment, Tilly looked crestfallen. Her mother wiped her buttery mouth with her bib, which made her change from crestfallen to indignant.

"Anyway, girls go to school," she said.

"You're only three," said Sprout. "Isn't there any bread and butter?"

"I'm sorry, I'll cut some. I thought you'd like the toast while it was hot."

"I did," said Sprout. "Can I have a yogurt while I'm waiting?"

His mother went to the refrigerator and gave Sprout a raspberry yogurt.

"I want one, too," said Tilly.

"I don't think you really do. You didn't finish it yesterday."

"I do, I do!"

"Oh, shut up," muttered Sprout. He knew that Tilly just wanted to copy him in everything, which was silly. He had once tried to explain to her that she would never catch up with him because by the time she was seven, as he was now, he would be eleven. Two figures. So she might as well stop trying to copy.

But Tilly hadn't understood any of this, so Sprout had given up. He had never gone in for explaining things, anyway. Either people understood or they didn't; and if they didn't, it was best to take some crackers, or a cookie, or both, and go away.

"Here you are," said his mother. She put a plate of thick brown bread and butter on the table. "Jam or marmalade?"

"Marmalade first," said Sprout.

"Please."

"Please," he repeated, with his knife already in the jar.

Tilly nibbled her toast and gazed at him while he ate one piece of bread after another until the plate was empty.

Then he had Swiss cheese and finished off with an apple.

"Do you know what?" Tilly said slowly and admiringly. "Sprout *stuffs* !"

"He's just got a big appetite," said their mother. "Besides, it's cold weather. People need more then."

"Sprout needs more all the time," said Tilly. She wasn't accusing; she was just proud, as if he were a very big prize pet.

"What did they have for lunch today?" Sprout's mother asked him. She knew it was the only question about school that he could be bothered to answer. She had long ago given up asking about arithmetic, or what they were reading, or whether Miss Price had been pleased with his picture of an igloo. Sprout was not really interested in any of these things; for him, school was just what had to go on between his breakfast and mid-morning milk and his lunch and coming home to tea.

"Hamburgers," he said. "Potatoes. Carrots. Chocolate pudding."

"Well, that sounds like quite a nice filling hot meal for a cold day."

"Custard," said Sprout.

"I had custard, too," Tilly boasted.

"I hope you didn't go and eat poor Raymond's hamburger as well, today," said Sprout's mother.

"He didn't want it," said Sprout. "And Moira didn't want her pudding. Neither did Graham."

"Sprout! Really, I don't know where you put it all!"

"Can I get down? Anyway, they were glad," said Sprout placidly. "Moira even gave me a licorice stick," he added. "So you can tell how glad *she* was."

"Can I get down, too?" squeaked Tilly, and fell off her stool. The kitchen floor was tiled, and she had hit her head, so she began to howl. Sprout stumped out of the room. Tilly was always falling off something, and often howling. He disliked the noise very much, and always went away until it was over. His mother had once said that she was afraid Tilly was accident-prone.

"What's that?" Sprout had asked.

"The sort of person who, if they can have an accident, they do," his mother had shouted through that particular fit of howls. It was when Tilly had sat on a bee. Sprout saw what his mother meant; with the whole lawn to sit on, Tilly had to go and choose a bee.

But that was a long time ago, in the summer; now it was winter, and dark outside when they had tea, and still darkish in the morning when he cycled to school. His friend Raymond had only seen two winters in England, and they had both been mild ones; so now, Raymond was always shivering and asking, "Will it get even colder than this?"

Raymond had been brought up in a hot country, near some jungle. Burma. With real elephants. Sprout envied Raymond very much indeed, but he pitied him in other ways. For being so cold, for instance, on what was really an ordinary November day. For looking so thin and yellow—the chillier, the yellower—whereas Sprout's face just turned from pink to nearly red. And Raymond, having known only those two unusually warm English winters, had never even seen snow.

"Don't they ever have it in the jungle, not even at Christmas?" asked Sprout.

"The last Christmas we were there, it was so hot we had to lie down indoors all afternoon."

"Even Tilly's seen snow," said Sprout. "Some fell off the roof onto her head when she was in her carriage. She howled."

"I hope it snows this Christmas," Raymond said.

Sprout said so did he; but privately, he wondered how Raymond would stand up to a real snowball fight.

"You ought to eat more," he said. "My mother says eating keeps people warm." He pitied Raymond still more when he found out that he had never even heard of fruitcake.

But Christmas was still a long way away. Sprout knew it wasn't even December yet. He sighed. Once tea was over, the evenings seemed long and rather pointless. In the summer, Raymond generally came over, or he went to Raymond's, just down the street. But Sprout's mother wouldn't let him out alone after dark, and Raymond's mother was frightened about Raymond going out into the cold at all; so Sprout was thrown back on the elephants, or on TV.

He had collected elephants ever since he could remember. Now he decided to bring them all down-stairs and let them watch the news. He turned it on very loud, to drown out the noise of Tilly, which was still going on. But the news was very boring, so to cheer the elephants up he gave them each a cookie out of the jar on the sideboard. There were seven ele-phants, so Sprout's mouth was very full indeed when his mother suddenly opened the living room door and let in the minister.

"Turn that sound down!" she shouted. Sprout switched off the TV set. Tilly had stopped crying at last and was giving the minister a curious stare.

"Well, well, well," he said heartily, "I'm glad to find this young man in, at any rate. So far, I haven't had much luck."

Sprout looked at him with a blank and bulging face.

"Sprout! Whatever are you eating now?" asked his mother. "The minister's come to ask if you'd like to be in the choir. At the church," she added with a reproachful glance, as if to say that church and cookies didn't go together at all.

But the minister patted Sprout's tuft and said, "Never mind, I won't ask him to sing now. The thing is, we do want to swell the choir a bit before Christmas." He looked kindly at Sprout's well-filled sweater. "Well, young man, think you could pipe up a few hymns on Sunday mornings?"

Sprout was still too full to do anything but blink.

"He can *whistle* quite well," said his mother doubtfully. In fact, she had never heard him sing anything but "Happy Birthday to You" once for each of Tilly's three birthdays. And Sprout had been in too much of a hurry to see them cut the birthday cakes than to bother with proper singing.

"Well, if he can keep a tune one way, he can keep it another," said the minister cheerfully.

Sprout swallowed the third cookie and managed to say through the other four, "Would I have to wear a white thing?"

"A surplice? We would have to try to find one to fit you, wouldn't we?" The minister cocked an eye at Sprout's short square figure, almost as broad as it was high.

Sprout looked gloomy. "They have frills around their necks," he said. "I've seen them," he added, as if challenging the minister to deny it.

"Well, yes, the boys do wear—"

"I'd look silly," said Sprout.

"Nonsense, you'd look very nice," his mother put in hastily.

"You'd get used to it," the minister smiled. "Besides, there's the carol-singing, I'm sure you'd enjoy that. No frills or surplices then!"

"What carol-singing?" Sprout asked cautiously.

"On Christmas Eve. It's a lot of fun. Last year they collected over ten dollars." Sprout looked up. "For the Organ Fund," the minister went on. Sprout looked down. "And I imagine you know some carols already, don't you?"

"Silent Night," muttered Sprout.

"There you are, then. Splendid!"

By now Sprout looked less bulging, but still blank. He had never thought "Silent Night" was particularly splendid.

"We go all around the neighborhood," said the minister, "and we have mince pies afterwards."

"Mince pies?" said Sprout. He stood stock-still.

"Yes, and coffee. We all gather at the organist's house, and his wife provides the food. It can be chilly work, you know, a couple of hours out there on a frosty night —"

"Did you say mince pies?" Sprout's square pink face had gone a shade pinker.

"That's right; very good ones she makes, too. Anyway, maybe you'd like to think about joining us. I must be leaving. I have several other houses to call on . . ."

"I'll join," said Sprout.

"Really, Sprout! . . . " began his mother; but the minister was saying "Splendid," and Tilly was squeaking "Me too!" and there was no time then to tell Sprout that you didn't join choirs just for mince pies.

Besides, if you were Sprout, that was exactly what you did.

The next day, at school, he told Raymond.

"I don't like mince pies," said Raymond. Sprout gazed at him in pity and astonishment.

"My mother once tried to make them," Raymond explained. "But she couldn't."

"Why not?"

"I don't know. They went all hard and black. We had to throw them away. She didn't have to cook anything in the jungle," he added by way of excuse for his mother, seeing Sprout's horrified frown. "Burmese boys did our cooking; and they never made mince pies."

Sprout thought that, apart from having met real elephants, Raymond's life seemed to have been extraordinarily bleak. And he didn't even bring anything to eat with his mid-morning milk, except once one very small brown banana, which Sprout had had to eat up for him during Geography, because he couldn't get through it. Sprout always brought at least two peanut-butter sandwiches, a couple of cookies, several crackers, and an apple. He looked forward to these all through the first two lessons.

On this particular day, Miss Price started them off with Arithmetic. One of the questions was about how much change you would get if you bought a pound and a half of cheese with a fifty-cent piece, and it cost twenty cents a pound. Sprout's mouth watered. Then they went on to History, and that was about Henry the Eighth and how he had huge banquets and picked up pieces of chicken and meat in his fingers. Moira said, "Ugh!" and Raymond looked disgusted, but Sprout didn't see that it was any worse than Tilly. Except that he supposed Henry the Eighth didn't wear bibs. By the time it was nearly eleven o'clock, Sprout could smell roast chicken so vividly that he almost knocked Graham over in his hurry to get out to his bicycle basket and those peanut-butter sandwiches.

They weren't a banquet, but they were better than nothing.

And then a very strange thing happened.

Sprout was leaning over the low school wall, watching the cars go by while the other children were kicking their ball around the asphalt playground. He never could understand why they ate so little and kicked so much. They seemed to have no idea what recess was for. But maybe their mothers were mean, or poor, and didn't let them bring decent food. He knew that this wasn't true about Raymond, whose mother was always sighing, "I do wish you ate like Sprout!" But Raymond was just naturally bleak and thin. Sprout was in a way sorry, and in a way glad; at least it meant that he always got double if they went to tea with each other. With the paper bag balanced carefully on the top of the wall, he took out the second sandwich. Then, suddenly, he didn't want it.

Sprout frowned. He looked at the sandwich; he looked in the bag. There were still the cookies to go, and the crackers, and. . . . He gazed at the sandwich again. It was a very funny thing. He just didn't seem to be able to put it in his mouth. He had never felt that way about a sandwich before. He was puzzled; he was surprised; everything, even the wall, even the playground, suddenly seemed quite strange.

Just as he was thinking this, the ball sailed past his head, over the wall, and down into the road. Sprout didn't pay much attention. It often happened. Someone would rush out and get it, as soon as there wasn't a car going by. Sprout had sometimes been surprised that they bothered to go on playing this game, day after day, when it meant that they had to go rushing out into the busy road instead of leaning peacefully against the wall and eating.

But now he was much more surprised about his sandwich. Here he was, holding it in his hand and not wanting to eat it.

Vaguely, in the middle of his bewilderment, he saw Raymond tear out into the road after the ball. This was unusual; generally one of the the bigger boys went. Sprout heard the squeal of brakes. He forgot the sandwich; he even dropped it. Then he saw Raymond lying flat on his face in the road.

There was a hush, then a hubbub. The boys shouted, and the girls screamed.

"Raymond's been run over!"

Within seconds, Miss Price had rushed out. Within minutes, an ambulance had arrived, and Raymond, a paler yellow than ever, was being lifted into it on a stretcher.

"Broke his leg!" said one boy.

"His arm!" said another.

"His back!" said Moira, goggling.

"Both his legs!" Graham suggested, trying to make up for coming in last.

Sprout stared at them all with a glazed expression. He had been shocked by the accident; but, unlike them, he had been shocked before it, too.

Slowly he walked over to his bicycle basket and put back the cookies and the crackers and the apple.

When the bell rang, he went in and sat through Penmanship and English and Geography, trying to think, as he alway did, "I wonder what's for lunch?"

But when it came to lunchtime, he not only refused to eat Moira's fish or Graham's plums; he couldn't even finish his own.

And when he got home to tea, and his mother announced: "Hot buttered toast!" all he did was sit and look at it. His mother was amazed. To make matters worse, Tilly just sat and looked at hers, too; copying Sprout, as usual.

His mother went so far as to question him about what had happened at school that day, and he told her of Raymond's accident.

"Oh!" she said, and in spite of her concern about Raymond, her face cleared a little. "I expect that's why you've lost your appetite!" She looked fondly at Sprout. "It would take away mine, too," she said sympathetically, "seeing a thing like that. Why didn't you tell me before? I've got to call his mother and find out the news."

She came back from the telephone smiling.

"It's all right. Only a sprained ankle and shock. So you can breathe again."

"I've been breathing all the time," said Sprout dully.

"No, I mean you can stop worrying. Look, that toast's gotten cold; I'll make some more."

"I don't want any," said Sprout. His mother stared at him, and he stared back; he was as amazed as she was. "I didn't want my sandwich, either," he said.

"When?"

"Before the accident."

Then Sprout's mother was really worried. "You'd better go up to bed," she said.

And without another word, Sprout did.

2

"Nothing to worry about," said his father breezily the next day. "He's probably just got a chill."

But Sprout's mother knew that it would take more than a chill to make Sprout lose his appetite for a whole day. Or even a whole hour. He had had chills before, and mumps, and chicken pox, but he had never really lost his appetite. Even with whooping cough, he had managed to eat between the whoops. He had had measles, too, and astonished the doctor by eating three slices of bread and honey while his mother was fetching a glass of water so that he could take his pills.

"I'm not sure that he'll need them after all," the doctor had said; but Sprout had thought he might as well try one. Then he had eaten a piece of cake to take the taste away.

He always rather enjoyed being in bed with things like measles because people brought up all sorts of extras and seemed pleased when he ate them up. Grapes. Candy. Hard-boiled eggs. Buttered bread. Homemade biscuits.

But this time, it was different. There had been a dish of grapes by his bedside for nearly a whole day, and he hadn't eaten one of them. He couldn't understand it. Neither could his mother.

"He hasn't even got a temperature," he heard her saying to Mrs. Chad, whose day it was. Mrs. Chad came once a week to help do the floors. Before she went home, she stuck her head in at Sprout's bedroom door to say good-bye.

"I won't come in," she said, "in case it's anything catching. It's not myself, it's Albina I'm thinking of. That child'd catch a germ if it was sprinting from here to Peru." Albina was Mrs. Chad's little girl, who spent most of her time away from school ill. Mrs. Chad herself was always fat and pink; perhaps that was one reason why she and Sprout liked each other.

"What's all this about you going off your food?" she went on. "That won't do. What am I going to tell Albina at teatime? Only way I can get her to eat is to give her a catalog of what you've gotten through. She doesn't always believe it, of course, but then." Mrs. Chad often ended speeches with "but then." Sprout

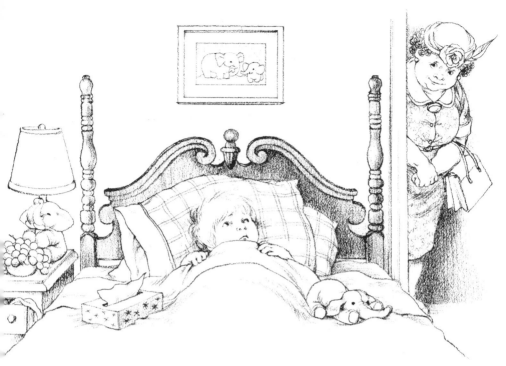

realized that she was another person who didn't see
any point in saying what was obvious. He blinked and
gave her rather a weak smile.

"Oh well, good-bye," she said, "and don't go
dieting. Think of me!"

Sprout heard her thump her way downstairs; then
he heard her talking to his mother for a while before
she left. He sighed. He was bored, but not interested
enough to listen. He looked at the grapes and sighed
again. He wasn't even interested enough to pull one
off its stalk, let alone eat it. "What a waste of grapes,"
he thought. What a waste of being in bed. It was all
very strange.

He must have gone to sleep, because it was dark
when the doctor came.

"I wouldn't have called you out," he heard his mother saying, "only it's so unlike him. And then my Mrs. Chad said . . ."

The doctor took Sprout's temperature. "I think your Mrs. Chad was right," he said. "This is the third case I've had today. Keep him warm. Light diet. Let me know if there are any further developments. I'll call again later in the week. Cheer up, young man"— he ruffled Sprout's tuft—"I don't think you'll fade away. You've got quite a bit on you to keep you going, haven't you?" And he gave Sprout a playful punch through the bedclothes.

His mother showed the doctor out. "What did Mrs. Chad say?" Sprout asked her when she came back.

"Flu," said his mother. "Now suppose you try to drink this milk."

Sprout tried. "Funny kind of flu," he said as he handed back the full mug.

"As a matter of fact, it is." His mother looked worried. "Never mind, you'll be able to eat all sorts of nice things as soon as your temperature's gone down."

"I thought it *was* down."

"It was. But with this sort of flu it can be down one minute and up the next."

"Like with my sandwiches. First I wanted one, and then I didn't."

"Yes, well I expect you'll want a lot again soon." His mother tucked in his top sheet.

Sprout slept. Sometimes he woke up just enough to hear Tilly squeaking in the distance, "I want flu, too!"

Then he turned over and went to sleep again. Sprout never did things by halves. In fact, he slept for nearly three whole days. But it might just as well have been three weeks, he felt when he finally woke up.

"What day is it?"

"Saturday." His mother was bending over him with something in a glass. "The doctor says you're to drink this."

"What Saturday?" Sprout blinked. "We haven't had Christmas, have we?"

"No, no," his mother smiled. "Not yet. You've just had a very nasty dose of the flu. You'll be up and around by Christmas all right."

Sprout lay looking at the ceiling. Gradually, things came back to him.

"What about that carol-singing?" he said. "We were going to have mince pies."

"Well, we'll have to see." Sprout frowned. He never liked it when his mother said that. He liked people to be definite: Yes or No.

"But Raymond's going," he said. "Isn't he?"

"I don't know. It depends on his ankle. He's still in bed. His mother and I have been calling each other up every day, to see how you both were."

Sprout had almost forgotten Raymond's accident. It seemed very unreal, very far away.

"Anyway, I shall go," he said. "How are the elephants?"

His mother assured him that the elephants were all right. She was glad to change the subject because, privately, she thought that Sprout would not go carol-singing unless he was a very different Sprout from the one who lay there now. Even in these few days, he had altered. His face was white, not pink. Oblong, not square. Only the sprout on top of his head was the same. In fact, it looked more sprout-like than ever, because he hadn't been well enough for anybody even to try to brush it down.

Sprout was a sad sight.

And he went on being a sad sight, even after the doctor had said he could get up. For he still had no appetite. His shirts hung loose on him, instead of bulging at the front; his jeans were baggy, and the snap at the waist never popped open any more after

meals. The only consolation was that his mother said he had better not go back to school yet.

Raymond hadn't gone back either; his ankle seemed to be a long time getting better.

December had come, and they hadn't seen each other for weeks. Sprout was bored stiff, and Tilly didn't make things any better by saying over and over: "I've gone off my food, too," as if it was something to be proud of. Their mother was worried, and a lot of boiled eggs got thrown away half-eaten.

"You're nearly as bad as Albina," said Mrs. Chad. She was sloshing around the kitchen floor; it would be her last floor-cleaning before Christmas. Albina, as pin-like as her mother was fat, lurked between the wet patches. Being away from school and not eating were nothing unusual for her.

"We're having a visitor for Christmas," she told Sprout. He was not at all interested. "My Dad says *he'll* eat a lot," she added. "Make up for me, my Dad says." Sprout looked blank with boredom.

"Look out," said Mrs. Chad. "Get your feet wet, my girl, and you'll be down with pneumonia." She shoved Albina aside; she had been sloshing too hard to listen.

"My Dad's going to pick him up in the patrol car," Albina went on defiantly. This, at least, would impress Sprout. He had always been envious that her father was a policeman and actually drove a police car.

"Lucky visitor," he said. He felt that to have a ride in a police car would almost make it worthwhile spending Christmas with the Chads.

The next day, the minister called.

"Oh no, I really don't think he should come," Sprout heard his mother saying on the phone. "He's hardly been out yet at all. No, I don't dare risk it."

"Risk what?" Sprout asked as she hung up.

"You going on that carol-singing. Next week."

"Is next week Christmas Eve?" Sprout had lost all track of time.

"Yes, and they're not starting until six o'clock. It'll be dark and cold. You certainly won't be up to it."

"I will!" said Sprout. "I want to!" He suddenly felt some of his old determination coming back. "They're having mince pies," he added, and his eyes went beady. He actually looked quite eager again.

"Yes, but I don't suppose you'd eat them," his mother said gloomily.

"I would, I would!" Sprout was almost bursting with indignation. "You promised I could go!" he said. There were tears of angry disappointment in his eyes.

His mother sighed. It was too bad, she admitted, but think of poor Raymond. He wouldn't be able to go either; his mother would never let him go out on the streets with that ankle.

Sprout's mouth went very straight and tight.

"You promised," he said.

And he stumped about with a straight, tight mouth for the next two days, saying very little at all except "You promised," whenever his mother wanted him to do something especially boring, such as wash.

By the third day, she was beginning to wonder.

"I don't know—maybe it'd do him good," she said to his father anxiously. "Maybe it'd even get him back on his food again."

"Might easily," said his father, who was never so anxious as his mother, anyway. "You don't want to coddle him. Good long walk in the cold air wouldn't do him any harm, if he was well wrapped up."

"But he hasn't got a really warm coat. That last year's one, I thought it'd see him through the winter, but he seems to have grown so. The sleeves hardly come below his elbows."

"Well then, for goodness sake!" said his father. "If *that's* all that's worrying you . . ."

Sprout's mother said it wasn't all, by any means. But then Sprout came into the room with such a tight mouth and such a "You promised" look on his face that she said no more. Sprout had a way of getting an idea and sticking to it until something had to happen.

What happened this time was that his father came home the next day with a huge brown paper box.

"What's that?" asked Sprout.

"Open it and see."

Sprout stared. "But it's not Christmas yet."

"Never mind."

So Sprout opened the box. Inside was something navy blue. Very thick, very heavy. He pulled it out.

"A duffel coat!"

"Looks like it, doesn't it?" grinned his father.

"But it's just like yours!" Sprout was beaming as he had not beamed for weeks.

"That's right. Go on and try it on."

"It's all stiff, Look, it nearly stands up by itself."

"It'll stand up better with you in it," said his father, and helped him with the sleeves.

"A regular grown-up duffel coat!" gasped Sprout,

struggling. He had always wanted one and had always had to put up with either a raincoat or a tweed coat, because his mother had thought these could eventually be passed down to Tilly.

But this coat had wooden closings, and was so big that it nearly reached his ankles. The cuffs had to be turned up twice before he could even find his hands. His father always did buy things on the large side. But Sprout didn't mind; he just stood there like a navy blue tent with a tuft on top and beamed.

"*Now* can I go carol-singing?" he asked.

And before he had time to add an accusing "You promised," his father had pulled the hood of the coat over his head and was saying, "We shall have to see" in a way that Sprout didn't mind at all. He knew that they had seen and that he would go.

"Can I go and show it to Raymond?" he asked.

"It seems a bit unfair," his mother pointed out, "if he's not allowed to go carol-singing and you are."

Sprout paused. "All right," he said. "I'll *make* him be allowed to go."

So he went in the new coat to see Raymond, who looked thinner and yellower than ever. Next to him, Sprout still seemed very well-covered indeed, especially in the coat. Raymond's ankle was wrapped in a bandage.

"Of course I want to come," he said, "but I can't."

"You can hobble, can't you?"

"Only a little. My mother keeps telling me to rest it. I'm fed up with resting!" said Raymond with sudden vigor. "I'd rather be back at school!"

Sprout gazed at him. "He must be really very fed up," he thought, "to say a thing like that." But it was understandable. Raymond lived in a top apartment alone with his mother; his father was still in Burma; he had no brothers or sisters, not even a Tilly; and his mother kept getting headaches.

"You're lucky," he said bleakly to Sprout. "I didn't think either of us would be going carol-singing, and now it's only me who's not."

Sprout understood this, too; he would have been very upset if it had been the other way around. Then he had an idea.

"Somebody could give you a piggyback," he said brightly.

"What's a piggyback?"

Really, for someone who had been in the jungle, it was surprising the things Raymond didn't know. Sprout explained.

"Oh, you mean like having bearers," said Raymond. Then it was he who had to explain to Sprout about natives carrying things—and sometimes people—on journeys.

"Yes, only it wouldn't be a native," said Sprout. "It might be the minister." After all, it was the minister who had wanted them to go, and he was large and hefty, and Raymond was small and light, so why not?

Just then Raymond's phone rang, and his mother came in to answer it.

"That might be him now," said Sprout. And strangely enough, it was. Sprout heard Raymond's mother saying the same things Sprout's own mother had said, only more tonelessly.

"No, he can't possibly . . . oh no, out of the question . . . yes, I'm sorry, too, but—"

"I want to speak to him," said Sprout. Suddenly Raymond's mother saw a stiff navy-blue figure standing right under her nose. She was a nervous person at the best of times, and now she was limp after a headache. She nearly dropped the phone.

"Hello," said Sprout into it. "He could come if you carried him piggyback."

There was a surprised pause at the other end.

3

The members of the choir were all different shapes and sizes. Some of them were stuffed into quilted parkas, some had ski masks, some thick scarves and knitted caps. Sprout was the shortest person there, but he didn't see anyone with such a good big duffel coat. The others all carried flashlights with disks of red paper stuck in the end, so that the procession down the road looked like a string of little red eyes. The minister had given out these bits of paper when they met at the church hall. Everyone had one except Raymond and Sprout. They hadn't brought flashlights because the minister had forgotten to tell them.

"Who's that?" asked the minister.

"Me," said Sprout. "I've got a new coat, so I'm coming, and if you give Raymond a piggyback, he could come, too. He's never even *had* a real mince pie!" he added hotly. "Only rotten black ones!" He made it sound as if the minister was joining in a plot to keep Raymond away from them forever.

No one, not even the minister, could hold out when Sprout was really determined. His voice became gruff, his face went pink, and his hair stood up more obstinately than usual. Of course, the minister couldn't see the face or the hair; but as soon as he realized who Sprout was, he remembered them. How could anyone forget?

So it was arranged. Sprout left Raymond's mother dazedly protesting, and Raymond looking surprised but gleeful.

"I bet nobody's ever gone carol-singing piggyback on a minister!" he said.

"See you on Christmas Eve," said Sprout. And he stumped home with his hood up and his hands deep down in the great stiff navy-blue pockets. They would hold a lot, he thought, those pockets. He was very proud of them. He was very proud of the whole duffel coat. And he was quite proud of himself, for having got everything so well fixed up.

"Oh dear, I hope no harm comes of it," said his mother.

"What could?" demanded Sprout, and went to see his elephants without waiting for an answer.

"I'm sorry," he said. "I should have remembered. Of course, the others have all been carol-singing before, so they knew. Still, don't worry, just keep all together. Well, *you've* got no choice, have you?" he added to Raymond, who was sitting on a table waiting for his ride.

Sprout was rather disappointed about not having a flashlight, but the coat made up for it. He swaggered along thinking how even the bitterest wind couldn't get through that. He could go to the North Pole in it and still be all right. He also thought that if he were Raymond, he would feel rather ashamed to have to be carried, but Raymond didn't seem to mind at all. He was highly flattered to have the minister as his bearer, and very happy to be with the party, anyway. The minister seemed happy, too.

"First time I've ever done this," he said merrily. "I feel like Good King Wenceslas himself!"

Sprout remembered that Good King Wenceslas had the page treading in his footsteps, not riding piggy-back, but nobody corrected the minister, so he just plodded on in contented silence. It was good, being out in the dark without anybody saying "Mind that puddle," or "Wait for Tilly." Of course, Tilly had wanted to come carol-singing, too, and hearing her wails as he left the house had made him feel all the more glad to be out.

"I can see over people's garden walls," said Raymond. He looked like a big dark bird, swaying against the sky up there on the minister's shoulder. "I wonder if it'll snow," he said.

"The forecast said it might," grunted the minister. He wouldn't have liked to admit it, but he was already getting rather out of breath. Raymond was light, but the rest of the choir were clumping along at a fast pace.

"Wait! Whoa! We'll stop here!" he called out. The others turned and straggled back.

"We usually start by the Church," said a voice in the dark.

"Never sung at this house before," remarked another.

"What's it matter?" said the minister. "All the better. Time we did. All right if I put you down for a minute, young man?" And he let Raymond gently down in front of a gate.

They all gathered around in front of a tall, thin house that loomed entirely black except for one light in the basement. Sprout didn't think it looked like a very good house to sing carols to, but the others were all shuffling up the path, so he shuffled with them. The minister helped Raymond up the steps to the porch and told him and Sprout to stand in front because they were the smallest.

"Right," he said. " 'Hark the Herald.' LAH!" He hummed the first note so loudly that Sprout nearly jumped out of his coat. Then the choir started up, and Sprout put in a "Hark the herald angels sing" whenever he could; the others all had the words on pieces of paper which they held under the beam of their red flashlights.

They were just starting the second verse when the front door opened. Sprout's nose had been almost

pressed against it, and it opened so suddenly that he fell flat on his face on the doormat.

He saw a pair of furry slippers, and a voice said, "No good you singing here. There's nobody in."

Sprout picked himself up. "There is. *You* are," he said. He thought that was obvious; if she hadn't been, he wouldn't have fallen over. He saw now that the fur-edged slippers were the bottom end of an old lady; the top end looked very cross indeed.

"Don't be fresh," she snapped. "I'm only the dogsitter. What's more, I've just lost the dog I'm supposed to be sitting with!"

"I'm sorry . . . " began the minister.

"He must've run out the back, and as if that's not bad enough, you've got to come singing carols at the front!"

"A dogsitter. That's funny," said Sprout. Of course, he knew about babysitters, but. . . .

"Funny!" the old lady croaked. "A pedigreed dog, high-strung, and you talk about funny! Go on, take your carols somewhere else; I've got to call the police!" And she slammed the door so violently that the choir scuttled down the steps with the minister behind them. He muttered "Merry Christmas" as he hastily picked up Raymond, who was only too glad to be carried away.

Sprout turned to scuttle, too, but something stopped him.

"Hey!" he called. The choir clumped down the path and out of the gate, chattering and giggling nervously about the old lady.

"Hey!" Sprout called again. "Wait for me! I'm stuck!"

The little red lights were proceeding down the road. "Never mind, keep going!" he heard the minister shout cheerfully.

But Sprout couldn't keep going. He could hardly even move. His duffel coat was caught in the door. It was so stiff, and stuck out so much, and he had been so far in the doorway, that the old lady had slammed it in.

Sprout pulled and tugged and yelled "Hey!" toward the disappearing red lights, but it was no good. He couldn't make them hear, and he couldn't get the coat out. And he was too short, and too stuck, to reach up for the knocker or the bell. His face grew pinker and pinker; his hair stood up in a desperate tuft. "Surely the carol-singers will miss me and come back," he thought. But they didn't; not even the minister. Sprout bitterly supposed he was too busy being a piggyback for Raymond.

There was only one thing to do. With fumbling fingers, Sprout struggled to unbutton the coat. He couldn't even manage this until he had taken off his woolen gloves; then at last, puffing and panting, he got each button undone and heaved himself out of the sleeves. He gave the coat a last violent tug with all his might, but it was absolutely wedged. And there he had to leave it, stuck in the door.

He decided not to knock now. The cross old lady would only be crosser than ever, and he had to hurry and find the choir. The longer he stayed there, the farther they would have gone. He was sure the minister would let one of them come back with him for his beautiful new coat. He was very sorry to leave it there; but if he didn't, he might never catch up with the choir at all. He might even miss the mince pies.

He ran out into the road and began to stump as fast as he could in the direction that the red lights had gone. Then he came to a corner, a crossroad. He looked left; he looked right; he looked straight ahead. There wasn't a red light to be seen. He listened. There wasn't a carol to be heard—only the sounds of faraway cars and somewhere a gate clicking as somebody hurried home out of the cold.

"That's funny," he thought. "Where can they have gone?" Then he remembered one of them saying something about the Crescent. He believed that was around to the right, so he stumped that way. On and on he went, but there seemed to be no Crescent, and there was certainly no choir. It must have been to the left, he thought; so he went back again and started from the crossroad in the opposite direction.

Still no choir. The streets were very empty, and the wind was cold. A flake of snow fell on Sprout's head. It stuck in his tuft like a crumb, but there was quite a nest of crumbs there before Sprout realized that it was snowing. He looked up as he passed a lamp post and saw hundreds of other flakes blowing out of the dark, through the light and into the dark again.

"Anyway, Raymond's got his snow," he thought. Then, the fact of there really being snow made him realize how cold he was. He had a thick sweater, and his corduroy jeans and rubber boots, but he missed that coat. Besides, the snow was getting into the tops of his boots.

And it came down thicker, and the wind blew harder, and his fastest stumping didn't seem to keep him anything but cold.

"They ought to have missed me by now," he muttered to himself. "Why aren't they out looking?" Raymond, at least, might have had the decency to notice that he wasn't there. It was all very well, being carried around like a hero, or some sort of mascot, and not even thinking of the person who had fixed things so that you could go at all. The colder Sprout became, the more cross he felt, and the crosser, the more miserable.

He had walked until his legs ached. There was snow on his chest and his shoulders; by now, his boots were half full of snow. He had to keep blinking the snow out of his eyes. What was more, it made the roads look different, so that when he tried to find his way back to that crossroad he had started from, he couldn't recognize it at all. None of these roads seemed familiar now; he must have taken a wrong turn.

"I'm lost," thought Sprout. He stood still for a moment, looking around to see if there was a policeman anywhere about. But there wasn't. Only snow. So he set off again; it was no good standing still. But with the next step he took, he wasn't even standing at all. His boot slipped on an icy patch, and he sat down with a thump. He was not only taken by surprise; he was quite hurt. His seat wasn't as well-covered as it used to be.

Sprout very rarely cried, but he felt like doing it now. He was lost, the choir was lost, his coat was lost, he was cold, and he had bumped himself. For a moment, he sat there with tears welling up; they probably would have come rolling down his cheeks, if he had not seen what he suddenly saw.

Standing right over him was a polar bear.

At least, that was what it looked like at a first snow-blind squint. Sprout blinked, and then the polar bear shook itself. For a moment, there was a blizzard.

Sprout was covered from head to foot, and through this frenzy of snow he heard a flapping noise which he recognized as ears. Not a polar bear's—their ears didn't flap.

When he had wiped the snow out of his eyes, he saw that what had been white was now gray. And what had been a polar bear was a dog.

A large, gray, shaggy dog, with a stumpy tail and a round face so covered in shag that there seemed to be no eyes there at all. But there were; from deep down under the damp hearth rug two black beads looked at Sprout.

"Hello," he said. The dog licked his nose. Its lick was warm and sent steam into the air.

"You've got fur," said Sprout grumpily. He felt that if he put out his own tongue, it would freeze. Anyway, he didn't much like being licked. He stood up.

"You'd better go home," he said to the dog. "Go on."

The buried black beads gazed at him. The dog didn't move, but its stump of a tail twitched with what looked like anxious hope.

"What's the matter?" asked Sprout. "Are you lost, too?"

The dog just stood there. Its stump stopped twitching and went down; but it did look very lost. Then Sprout remembered: the old lady dogsitter; the tall, thin black house; her saying she was going to call the police. . . .

"Hey," he said, "are you *that* dog?"

He felt sure it must be, and the thought cheered

him up. Perhaps they could help each other find the way home. And if he could get the dog back to the old lady, she would be pleased, and not so cross, and he would get his duffel coat back, too.

"Come on, then," he said, and put his numb hand through the dog's collar, which was thick and heavy with brass studs. He began to drag the dog along the road. At first, it didn't seem to be sure whether it wanted to come or not; but after Sprout had given it a few hefty heaves, it decided that it might as well, and padded along beside him quite trustfully. This was a good thing, because he could feel that it was a very strong dog and would have been hard to hold if it had chosen to go another way. Not that Sprout himself knew where they were going; but it must be somewhere, he thought hopefully. Having the dog beside him made him more hopeful than before. There were two of them now, which was better than being alone; and there was at least a little warmth for one of his hands in the thick fur where he was holding the collar.

"I should think you *would* get lost," he said, "with fur like that. You can't even see where you're going." He thought it was a shame to let a dog grow fur all over its eyes.

"No wonder you need a dogsitter," he said.

They plodded on, with Sprout's boots crunching, and the dog's paws rustling in the snow.

They came to a corner. "Now which way?" asked Sprout. The dog sniffed the cold, blowy air. Sprout screwed up his purple face. He didn't dare to sniff; he felt that if he did, his nose would fall off like a frozen button.

"Oh well, come on," he commanded the dog again, lugging it along toward the next lamp post. He was beginning to think he would never find that tall, thin house again; and the dog didn't seem to care much which way it went or to have any sense of direction. Sprout supposed it thought it was just out for a walk. He dragged its collar more firmly, to let it know that this was business, not pleasure. Any pleasure he had had about being out by himself at night was completely gone; he was rather peeved with the dog for seeming to be enjoying itself.

"Hurry up," he told it, "you'll have to walk faster than that." And he puffed and panted and stumbled half-blindly on—until suddenly he saw a sight that made his mouth drop wide open.

His own house! They were on his own road, and there was his own front gate and the light of his own front room—with the curtains not drawn—shining on to his own newly-snowed-upon front garden. Only it looked quite different, not like a garden anymore; just a great, smooth pad of snow.

Sprout could hardly believe his eyes. How he could not have recognized it all until now, he didn't know. He had simply been too cold, and too lost, and too anxious to move the dog along to notice anything properly for the last half mile.

"Hey, this is my house," he told the dog. "I meant to find yours, and I've found mine by mistake!"

The dog's black beads blinked expectantly somewhere underneath the carpet of its face. It pulled on its collar as if to say, "Come on, what are we stopping for?" It even tried to pull Sprout past his own front gate.

"Oh no you don't," he said. "We're going in here whether you like it or not." And he tightened his mouth and firmly dragged the dog up the side passageway, toward the back door and the kitchen.

As he came to the door, he did have one uncomfortable thought. What would his mother say when she saw him come home with a dog instead of a coat? If only he had found the dog's house first. Still, here they were, and at least he had *got* the dog. And he was too cold to think of anything much, except that it would be nice to be indoors and get the snow out of his boots.

He shoved open the back door, which led straight into the kitchen. He didn't bother to shut it; he hardly ever did, and now his only concern was to get himself and the dog inside.

His mother wasn't there, but Tilly was, in her bathrobe. Sprout was vaguely surprised at this; he knew it must be long past her bedtime.

"My hot-water bottle burst!" she announced proudly. "My sheets are wet, and all my blankets. What's that bear doing here?" She pointed at the dog. She seemed to be quite prepared for its being a bear.

"It's a dog, stupid," said Sprout. He had forgotten that he had once thought it was a bear himself. "Here, hold it," he added, as the dog tugged away from him. "I want to get my boots off."

Tilly delightedly took hold of the dog's collar, while Sprout bent to take off his first boot. A heap of snow landed on the kitchen floor. He was just hopping about, struggling with the second boot, when he heard a loud squeak. A yelp. A scuffle.

He looked around just in time to see Tilly's rabbit-eared slippers flying through the kitchen door. For one second, her fat, pink legs were in mid-air; the next second, they had gone. So had the dog.

4

Sprout padded to the back door in his cold, wet socks.

"Hey!" he shouted. "Where are you going? Come back!"

But the passageway at the side of the house was empty. Somewhere in the direction of the road, he heard Tilly squeaking; then that noise faded out, as if she had been whisked not only off her feet but beyond squeaking-distance.

Sprout stood there for a moment in blank dismay. He knew it was a strong dog; he knew it hadn't particularly wanted to come into his house; he knew that if he told Tilly to hold its collar, that was exactly what she would do, thinking she was being like him.

He also knew that if his mother came downstairs and found out what had happened, there would be a terrible fuss.

He thought of all these things very quickly and decided that he must get Tilly and the dog back at once. But he couldn't go out in just his socks. Behind him stood his boots and two puddles of melting snow. He looked desperately around and saw a pair of very old and shapeless shoes lying by the broom closet. They were Mrs. Chad's; she left them there to wear when she was cleaning floors. He put them on. They were much too big, but never mind. Coat? Too late. He wasn't sure where his old one was and there was no time to go rummaging around in the hall closet now. But hanging on the hook on the kitchen door was Mrs. Chad's large, flowered smock. He snatched it down and wrapped it around his shoulders. It was better than nothing.

He was just going to rush out when he had another idea; a really bright one. He dashed to the pantry—except that he couldn't really dash, as he discovered when he lost one of the shoes. Still, he shuffled there as quickly as possible, flung open the door, and muttered, "Good. Just what I wanted."

On the bottom pantry shelf, which was a marble slab, lay an enamel plate with two lamb chops on it. Sprout seized one of these chops and hurried out. He could hear his mother still thumping around upstairs, changing Tilly's bed. If he was very quick, he might be back before she came down. And the chop, he thought, might make him much quicker. He had seen that dog sniff when there had been nothing to sniff but snow. Now, if it sniffed meat, it would come his way, bringing Tilly with it. He had once seen a thing on TV, about police dogs and how they picked up scents; and he guessed that dog was hungry, anyway.

So out he went, keeping the shoes on as best he could, clutching the smock with one hand and the chop with the other.

But once in the road, which way to go? He looked up to the left and down to the right; there was no sign of Tilly or the dog. He called Tilly's name; no answer. He didn't know the dog's name, so he couldn't call that. It wasn't much use just yelling, "Dog!" He must trust to the chop. Then he remembered that dogs picked up scents along the ground. What he really needed was a piece of string.

And now he had his first bit of luck that evening. He put his hand into one of the pockets of Mrs. Chad's smock, not really very hopefully, but just in case. And there, to his surprise, was, not string, but the next best thing: a carefully rolled-up piece of long ribbon. It was one of Albina Chad's hair ribbons, he knew at once. Whenever she didn't wear a pink butterfly barrette, she wore a ribbon, tied to make a very skinny ponytail; there always seemed to be more ribbon than there was hair.

As far as Sprout could see in the dark, this looked like a white satin ribbon. He stopped for a moment under a lamp post and tied the ribbon around the chop. Then he shuffled on, trailing the chop along the snowy path. Twice it came off, and he had to retie it.

His fingers were so numb with cold that this was very difficult. And all the time he was getting more and more worried; his mother would certainly have come down by now and found Tilly gone and his boots there, and goodness knows what she would think.

He shuffled more quickly, down one road after another. Surely they couldn't have gotten very far. Even though it was a strong dog, Tilly was no lightweight, and it must soon get tired, having her dragging on its collar. But what if he was going in the wrong direction? How far could a dog smell? And would the snow freeze the smell out of the chop anyway? Sprout was beginning to be very worried indeed, when suddenly, something knocked him over.

"Help!" he spluttered, with his mouth full of snow. And then he saw what it was. The dog, with Tilly still on its collar, and with its teeth already in the chop. He grabbed its stumpy tail and clutched its long fur.

"It worked!" he exclaimed triumphantly. For a moment he forgot being cold, or falling over for the second time that night; he just felt like a very clever policeman.

"You idiot!" he turned on Tilly. "What did you want to go and let him run off for?" He held the dog tightly, but there was no need now. It was standing quite still. Only its jaws moved, chewing the chop.

"He took me," said Tilly. "He's a very quick dog. He took me for a walk." She looked very pleased with herself. "Now I'm out in the snow like you," she said.

"Well, you shouldn't be," said Sprout crossly. "You've only got your bathrobe on."

"I know whose *that* is." Tilly stared at the smock. "That's Mrs. Chad's. *And* those shoes," she added. "They're too big."

"Come on," commanded Sprout. "Home." There were times when Tilly had to be treated like a dog; but at least a dog didn't get lost *and* make silly remarks.

"Wait for Raymond," said Tilly.

"Raymond?" Sprout stared. "What are you talking about?"

"He's in there." Tilly looked toward a clump of black bushes in the entrance of a front drive; it was from this entrance that the dog had pounced.

"Don't be silly. He can't be. He's on the minister."

But just as he spoke, he saw a small, thin figure limping toward them.

"Hello," said Raymond. "Where have you been? They're all looking for you."

"All who?" Sprout was much too confused to think straight. After all, for someone who had lost his appetite after the flu, he had had a tiring evening.

"The choir. I kept telling them you weren't there. I kept saying 'Wait,' and they kept not waiting, and the minister said 'I imagine he's gone on in front,' and then you hadn't, and then he put me down."

"What for?"

"While he told the others what to do. Some had to go on singing, and some had to go back and look for you. But I bet they didn't. They wanted their mince pies. Anyway, while he was talking, I gave him the slip."

"The what?" Sprout was completely dazed. What with finding the dog, and then losing it, and then losing Tilly and finding her, and finding Raymond who wasn't supposed to be lost at all. . .

"I got away," said Raymond knowingly. "You get used to that sort of thing in the jungle. Slipping behind a tree, into the undergrowth. Keeping very quiet, so the animals won't hear you. They sometimes call it freezing," he added with pride.

"I've been freezing for hours," grumbled Sprout. "Why didn't you go on riding piggyback?"

"I wanted to track you. They do that out there, too. Tracking. I knew your boots had a star on the soles, so I thought if I could find some star-prints, they'd end up with you. But I didn't have a flashlight," he added sadly.

Sprout looked at Raymond with new respect. He

would never have believed his skinny little friend had so much go in him — adventure, even.

"What about your ankle?" he asked.

"He's finished it all up," announced Tilly, looking at the dog. "Even the bone."

"I was just giving it a rest," said Raymond. "And then *they* came along. I was taking cover under a bush. Then something came snuffling up."

"That was Daddy's supper," said Tilly. "Now what will he have?" She gazed at the dog, and its black beady eyes gazed back as if it expected another chop at any minute.

"Never mind," said Sprout impatiently. "Anyway, it's your fault. Now we've got to get back home. And there'll be a fuss."

"Whose dog is it?" asked Raymond. Sprout reminded him about the old lady and explained what had happened. "But it's no good, I couldn't find the house," he said. "Come on." He sighed gloomily. Everything had gone wrong. No carols, no coat, no mince pies — and trouble ahead.

"Wait a minute," said Raymond. "Wasn't it that tall, thin house, all black?"

"Yes. But I've looked and looked, and it's just not there."

"Don't be crazy," said Raymond. He sounded much more lively than usual. Perhaps he felt one up on Sprout because he was wearing ordinary clothes and not baggy shoes and a flowered smock. "I bet I could find it," he said. "I bet it's not far away. In the jungle, you have to learn to find places much farther away than that."

"This isn't the jungle," replied Sprout. He looked bleakly at the snowy street.

"No, but we can pretend it is. And anyway, that house can't be far, because I was near it when the minister put me down, and I can't have walked very far because of my bad ankle. As a matter of fact, I rested in several bushes," he admitted. "I was being a wounded native."

Sprout stared at him harder than ever. This was quite a new Raymond; new to him, at any rate. Perhaps getting run over had perked him up. Raymond had often talked about the jungle, but he had never acted it before. Now he stood there with eyes as bright and black as the dog's, only not buried in fur, and he hopped up and down on his good ankle and said, "Isn't it great, real snow! It's even better for tracking in than mud."

"But we've got to go home," said Sprout.

"Let's take the dog back first."

"I'll be in enough trouble as it is."

"But listen, that house is on the way home, anyway."

Sprout looked at him very doubtfully. "You don't know," he said.

"I bet it is. Anyway, I bet it's nearer here than home is. It must be, because I told you, I couldn't have walked far."

"He's eating the string now," said Tilly.

Sprout looked at the dog and dragged Albina's ribbon out of its mouth.

"Come on," said Raymond. "Let's start tracking."

"Tilly can't," Sprout said. "She's got to go home."

"I don't want to!" Tilly began to wail.

"All right, then," said Raymond. "I'll take the dog and you take her. I'll find that house, you'll see. I might even get a reward," he added with a glint in his eye.

"I want to come!" Tilly squeaked in her most protesting way. "I like this snow. *And* I like this dog!" She showed signs of really howling.

Sprout stood for a moment, uncertain. He didn't see why it should be Raymond who took the dog back, after all he himself had been through; and he couldn't stand the noise Tilly was obviously going to make.

"All right," he said. "Only we'll have to be quick."

"I can't be, very," said Raymond. "But I can track. Look, there are my footsteps, where I came. You can tell, because one's a whole foot and the other's just a toe."

Sprout gazed at the marks in the snow under the light of a street lamp. There were other footprints too, but much bigger ones, and with both feet.

"Come on, then," he said. It was a good idea of Raymond's, to have limping footprints. Sprout followed them, holding the dog, to the next lamp; Raymond and Tilly staggered along behind.

"That's funny," Sprout said. "It looks as if they stop here. Maybe this is where the minister put you down."

"No," said Raymond, "that was by a big hedge. This is where I crossed the road."

"That's very naughty," piped up Tilly. "You mustn't cross roads."

"You mean *you* mustn't," Sprout said scornfully. "That's because you're only three." He felt rather ashamed of her and wished she wasn't there. He grabbed her by the bathrobe and lugged her across the road. The dog helped to pull them both, and Raymond hobbled behind as best he could.

"If this dog was a bit bigger," said Sprout, "you could have a ride."

"He looks strong enough," Raymond panted, "but too short. My knees would be on the ground."

"I want a ride!" said Tilly. "He's big enough for me!"

"You'd fall off," said Sprout. "You always do."

"I wouldn't, I wouldn't. . . "

Sprout thought that if she started to wail again, he would really give up. He was beginning to wonder if Raymond had any idea where they were going. The wind was blowing through Mrs. Chad's smock, and the shoes were hard to keep on. Besides, they were so full of snow that he might just as well have come out in his socks.

Raymond limped along, closely inspecting the ground. "Yes, these are all mine," he said. "I did all these." He seemed to be more interested in the actual footprints than in where they were leading. He peered at them with great satisfaction; he seemed to be carried away with the idea of tracking for tracking's sake. His nose was bent so close to the ground that he didn't even see what Sprout suddenly saw.

"Hey! There it is!"

"What?"

"My coat. Look, in that door. This is the place. This is it."

"You see?" said Raymond. "What did I tell you? I told you I'd find it."

"You didn't. I did," said Sprout. "You would have gone right past."

It was all very well, Raymond being so clever, but Sprout didn't see why he should get all the credit. If it hadn't been for the coat, they might not have felt absolutely sure it was the right house at all.

"I would have known that house anywhere," said Raymond airily.

Sprout didn't argue. He just said, "I know my coat," and started to march up the path.

"Why are we going in this house?" said Tilly. "This isn't our house."

"We know that," said Sprout. He wished again that Tilly wasn't there; she was so dumb. The dog seemed rather dumb, too; it didn't even show any sign of being glad to be home. "But at least," thought Sprout, "the old lady would be glad to see it. Very glad, after all this time." So much for the police: they couldn't have looked for it very well. Sprout was pleased to feel that he had outwitted them.

"You'd better stay behind me," he told Tilly. "She'll have a fit if she sees you like that." Raymond was still struggling up the front steps as Sprout knocked on the door.

"You see," said Raymond as he peered at the steps

in the dim light that shone up from the basement. "There's all the choir's footprints. *And* yours with the star. I told you so!"

"My coat's what marks the house," said Sprout flatly. Raymond's tracking was all very well, but it was he who had found the dog. And he was even inclined to think, now, that it had been rather clever of him to leave his coat in the door. Nothing could have made him more certain that this was the right house.

Just as he was about to knock a second time, the door opened. But this time it was only his coat that fell down, not him.

"Hello," he said. "That's my coat, and here's your dog." He gave the dog a shove forward toward the furry slippers and picked up the coat.

"Hey, take that animal off me!"

Sprout's mouth dropped open.

"But you said you were a dogsitter. And you lost the dog. And I found him."

Now the old lady's mouth dropped open.

"Dog? More like a hearth rug!" she said. "Anyway, mine's in, safe and sound. See for yourself. Ping-Pong!" she squawked.

There was a curious high-pitched yap, and Sprout's dog almost pulled him over with excitement. From behind the fur-edged slippers appeared a very small, bulgy-eyed Pekinese.

5

"Silly, you got the wrong dog," said Raymond.

Sprout stared from the big dog to the Pekinese, and all he could say was, "Yes." In fact, the dog he was holding could hardly have been more wrong. Wrong shape, wrong size — and then suddenly it gave what the old lady clearly thought was a very wrong bark. Compared with the Peke's, it was more like a roar.

"Take him away!" she gasped; she had nearly jumped out of her skin. "Ping-Pong! Where are you?"

But the Peke had scuttled off into the darkness of the hall behind her; and before Sprout could take a breath to speak, he wasn't holding the big dog anymore. It had given an almighty wrench and broken free. It nearly knocked the old lady flying as it rushed in after Ping-Pong.

"Now look what you've done! Get him back! Catch him! He'll kill her!"

"He won't," said Sprout. "Anyway, I can manage him." And he stumped straight into the house. Tilly and Raymond followed, but what with the hall being dark, and the old lady flustered, he didn't notice them.

Sprout saw the broad, matted back end of the big dog disappearing down some steep stairs. There was a tremendous din of high yapping and deep, cavernous barking. Sprout followed this din down the stairs and found himself in a large, brightly lit kitchen. But it was a kind of living room, too. There was a stove, and a TV set, and a wicker chair. On the floor in front of the stove was a green velvet cushion with gold tassels; and on this cushion, even by the time Sprout got there, sat the Peke. It was quivering but somehow queen-like, as if it was on its throne. It still yapped in a breathless way, as if to say "I was here first!" Its eyes bulged indignantly at the big dog, who looked at it, and then looked at the fire, and then sat down.

"There you are," said Sprout. "I told you he was all right." He beamed at the big dog. It had stopped barking and was sitting on the hearth rug with its black beads bright in the firelight.

"I don't know what's right about bringing him in here," snapped the old lady. "Dirty big sheep dog!"

"He's not dirty," Sprout retorted. "Just snowy."

"Well, the sooner you get him out, the better. Hey

aren't you the boy in the front of them carol-singers, the fresh one?"

But before Sprout had time to answer, there was another noise, much louder than the dogs. A great thud, and then an ear-splitting yell. Some scuffling, and more yells. Even Ping-Pong stopped in mid-yap.

"That's Tilly," said Sprout. "Falling downstairs."

"For goodness sake, whatever next?" The old lady rushed out of the room. She came back carrying the wailing Tilly, with one rabbit slipper and one bare foot. Raymond limped behind, holding the other slipper.

"She tripped over the ears," he explained.

"She always does," said Sprout. He went over to examine Tilly, who was now sitting on the old lady's knee in the wicker chair, still wailing. A big bump was already coming up on her forehead.

"Oh boy," sighed Sprout. "Another accident. Have you got a lollipop?"

"A what? Who is she? And what's she doing out on a night like this, with only her bathrobe on? Poor little thing!" She rocked Tilly back and forth. She suddenly

looked less cross and quite human. But then, "Who's this?" — she glared suspiciously at Raymond. He cowered and blinked in the bright light. He seemed to be reduced from a brave tracker to a frightened mouse.

"He's my friend," explained Sprout. "He was run over," he added, as if that made Raymond an important person, not to be glared at.

"When? Where? I don't know what all this is about, I don't know where you all come from, I don't know whether I'm on my head or my heels — there, dear," she broke off to comfort Tilly. "Never mind, then, ssh, you'll be all right, so you will."

"She would if you had a lollipop," said Sprout. Tilly was still wailing, but he could tell when her wails changed from real pain to just keeping it up. The keeping-it-up stage was what she had reached now. At the word "lollipop," she paused for breath and opened one eye. And as soon as she paused, the big dog got up, padded over, and licked her bare foot. Tilly's wail turned to a squeak, and the squeak to a giggle.

"That tickles!" she said.

"There!" said the old lady. "And who's a brave girl, then? And fell down all them nasty stairs?"

"I did," said Tilly. She was beginning to look pleased with herself. "Can I have a lollipop?"

"I'm sorry, dear, I don't think there's any lollipops — but I tell you what there *is*," she added hastily, as Tilly's face showed signs of going square and wet again. "You just sit there a minute and I'll fetch them out." She dumped Tilly in the wicker chair; the big dog went on licking Tilly's foot.

"He likes me," said Tilly. "He thinks I've got a nice taste."

"Well, 'Sugar and spice and all things nice, that's what little girls are made of,' eh?" said the old lady. She was poking around in a cupboard on the other side of the room.

"She'd better have her other slipper," muttered Raymond, and handed it to Sprout. They both felt slightly annoyed that the old lady was making such a fuss over Tilly; and Sprout was worried about getting home. He had imagined that he would just give back the dog, get back his coat, and go. And now everything was held up. And it wasn't even the right dog.

But then he saw what the old lady was bringing from the cupboard: a mince pie.

"Here," she said, "they left me this, in case I got hungry. They're very good—they always leave me something. Now, dear, don't you think you'd feel better with a piece of mince pie inside you?" She held out the plate to Tilly.

"That looks like a *proper* mince pie," Raymond said. He eyed the plate with interest and respect.

"Of course it's proper, what d'you think?" The old lady looked at him suspiciously.

"I've seen ones like that in shops," said Raymond, "but my mother wouldn't buy them. She said you never know what they put inside."

"Well, this doesn't come from any shop!" said the old lady indignantly. "And it's got good mincemeat inside, that's what! Wherever have *you* been brought up, then, I'd like to know? Anybody'd think you were a foreigner; 'proper mince pie,' indeed!"

"He's from the jungle," said Sprout.

"Well, near it," Raymond put in. He noticed that the old lady looked startled; perhaps she thought that to have been run over *and* in the jungle was a bit peculiar. Tilly took a piece of mince pie. So did the big dog.

"Hey," said the old lady, "that's not for you. Put it down!" But that piece had gone.

"It was his dessert," said Sprout. "He's had a chop already."

"He's got no business," began the old lady, "coming in here and — "

"Good!" said Tilly in a crumby squeak. She had
settled back comfortably in the wicker chair.

"We've got to go home," said Sprout. He stopped
looking at the mince pie, set his mouth in a firm line,
and stuck Tilly's other slipper on her foot. She kicked
it off again.

"It's nasty and cold," she said.

"Of course it is," the old lady said sympathetically.

"They both are. Come on, we'll put them down and
warm them by the stove. She'll catch her death!" she
said to Sprout, as if it was all his fault.

"I only wanted to bring back your dog," he said
glumly. "And then you hadn't even lost it."

"As to that," said the old lady, "first I had, and
then I hadn't. As soon as I came down to call the
police, there she was, sitting on that cushion, large as
life. And I'd searched the house, top to bottom. I
think she was just playing a game with me — weren't

you, Ping-Pong, my beauty, eh?" She smiled at the Peke, who goggled royally back.

"Look out," said Raymond, "he's going to take another piece." Sprout pulled the big dog away from the plate just in time.

"The sooner you take him away, the better," said the old lady. "But first you just tell me where this poor little thing lives, and I'll ring up her Mom. She must be worried out of her life; though what she was thinking of, letting a little child run out in the streets in that condition, I don't know. Children like you carol-singing, that's one thing. But my goodness, she can hardly be much older than my little granddaughter. In fact, they're very much alike; I thought so when I first picked her up. Well? D'you know her name and address. Or do I have to call the police after all?"

She looked quite fierce again. Sprout stared. It was clear that the old lady liked girls and not boys — and small dogs, not big ones. But he only now realized that she hadn't put him and Tilly together.

"She lives where I live," he said. "Her mother's my mother. She's Tilly."

"And he's Sprout," said Tilly. "And that's Raymond. I don't know who the big dog is. But I think he wants another piece of mince pie."

The old lady stared from Sprout to Tilly and back again. "Well!" she said. "I would never have thought it. Brother and sister! And her with all those curls!" She patted Tilly's head and looked unbelievingly at Sprout's straw-like tuft.

"I can't help it," he muttered. "Anyway, we've all got to go home."

"Can't I give him one more?" asked Tilly.

"No," said Sprout. "It's a waste." It wasn't that he begrudged the dog mince pie, but after all, it had had one piece already, and so had Tilly, and she seemed to be getting all her own way. "Come on," he said. "They're warm now." He picked up the slippers from the front of the stove.

"They're sopping wet," said the old lady. "You just tell me your Mom's number and I'll call her. My goodness, I should think she'll give you the dickens, taking your little sister out like that."

"I didn't," said Sprout. He said no more. For one thing, it was too complicated; and for another, he didn't want to get the dog into worse trouble. So he simply told the old lady his telephone number, which his mother had drummed into him years ago. His heart sank as she went to the phone. He saw a terrible fuss ahead.

"I wouldn't mind trying a piece," said Raymond, eyeing the mince pie. "I'm hungry."

"I'm not," said Sprout gloomily. He had thought he might be, after the carol-singing; but now he realized he wasn't. Even if he had found his coat, and a dog, and Tilly, and Raymond, he still hadn't found his appetite.

"That's funny, there's no answer," said the old lady. She put down the phone. "Are you sure that's the right number? You're not telling me a fib?" She looked suspiciously at Sprout; she clearly didn't trust him. This made him furious.

"Of course it is," he said with a very red face. "It always has been. Even *she* knows that," he nodded toward Tilly.

"All right, but in that case, your Mom's out."

"I imagine she's out looking," suggested Raymond timidly. "Or gone around to my mother to see."

"Well, you've got to get home somehow. Ping-Pong's people'd have a fit if they came back and found *him* here."

She looked disapprovingly at the big dog, who had now settled down by the stove with his chin on his paws.

"One thing they've always said: I'm never on any account to let any other dogs near Ping-Pong. And now look!"

"Ping-Pong doesn't seem to mind," said Sprout. In fact, the two dogs were lying side by side in perfect peace. Ping-Pong had evidently decided that as long as no one attacked her cushion, all was well.

"That's not the point. How do I know what he might give her? He might have mange, for all I know. Distemper. Fleas."

"He hasn't!" said Sprout indignantly. "All he's got is too much hair. He can't see where he's going. It's not his fault."

"Anyway, he's got to go somewhere, and so have you," insisted the old lady. "I'd better call a taxi."

"I went in a taxi once," piped up Tilly, sounding pleased.

"They cost a lot," said Sprout. He foresaw even more trouble.

"Never mind that; I'd pay my dog-sitting money to get that poor little thing back in her own bed safe and sound. Not that I'd *get* the money," the old lady added sharply, "if they found you all here. If they came in and saw that dog, I'd never sit again!" She picked up the telephone.

"A big black taxi," Tilly went on comfortably. "I had a lollipop in it. To make me not be sick. But I *was!*" Sprout glowered at her. That would really be the last straw.

"That you, Bert?" the old lady was saying into the telephone. "I've got a job for you. Here. Yes, and be quick about it. I'll tell you when I see you." She banged down the receiver and said with great relief, "That's all right. Bert'll be here any minute. So you'd better get your slippers on now, dear." She picked up the rabbits by their ears and wedged them onto Tilly.

"Who's Bert?" Sprout asked.

"The taxi. My nephew. He lives just around the corner. Which is lucky, seeing I sometimes have to sit with Ping-Pong until after midnight. Then Bert takes me home. Do anything for his old Auntie, will Bert. Now then, dear, let's see your bathrobe's wrapped around tight, that's it. . . . "

She fussed over Tilly, who was thoroughly happy and very proud of the bump on her forehead. Sprout and Raymond stood and waited in gloomy silence for Bert.

When he came, he turned out to be a round, pink

young man with a duffel coat like Sprout's — only older — very short, bristly hair, and very red sticking-out ears. Balanced over one of these was a sprig of mistletoe.

"Hello, Aunt May" he said cheerfully but respectfully. "What's the idea, fetching me out on Christmas Eve — *hello!*" He broke off in astonishment, taking in the assembly in the kitchen. "You didn't tell me you had company!"

"I haven't," snapped Auntie. "At least, I won't have, soon as you get going. You're to take them home. And what's more, you're to stay there till his Mom comes back." She nodded sharply toward Sprout. "You might find it's an empty house. In which case," she added severely, "this little dear here" — indicating Tilly — "is not to be left. You understand?"

"O.K. Aunt May" said Bert, looking bewildered. "Anything you say."

"Right. Off you go, then." The old lady picked Tilly out of the wicker chair and gave her a smacking kiss. "My little granddaughter all over again," she said fondly. And then, less fondly, to Sprout, "I suppose you can tell him the way."

"Number two, Penzance Gardens," said Sprout. He was very glad she hadn't kissed him. As for the way, he hoped Bert knew it. Bert said he did.

"What, that dog and all?" he said. He looked at the huge sheep dog with some misgiving.

"Certainly the dog," said Auntie. "And the quicker the better."

"He can sit with me," said Sprout.

"Is he yours?" Bert asked.

"No."

"Oh." Bert looked blank. "Well, then, where's *he* got to be dropped?"

"He hasn't," said Sprout. "He's . . ."

"Stop arguing," said the old lady. "Just take them home." Sprout was glad not to have to do any more explaining, and Bert said meekly, "All right." So they all went up the steep stairs and out to the taxi.

"And you come back here and tell me when you've done it!" Aunt May called after Bert from the front door.

Bert grinned at Sprout. "She's a bit of a Tartar, Aunt May is," he said out of the corner of his mouth. "Never mind; hop in."

He lifted Tilly up into the back seat. "How come she's in this gear?" he said. "Funny night to be out in your bathrobe."

"Can I sit in the front?" asked Sprout. He was holding the dog's collar with one hand — and Mrs. Chad's smock with the other — and thought this was no time to be discussing Tilly.

"Not with him, you can't," said Bert. "His paws might get in the works."

So Sprout hauled the dog into the back with Raymond and Tilly.

It had stopped snowing, but the roads were icy.

"I'll have to take it slow," Bert called over his shoulder. The old-fashioned black taxi started with a jerk. Tilly fell off her seat.

"Why don't you hold on?" said Sprout. He was afraid she might start howling again. But she didn't; after a moment of surprise, she just laughed.

"That was funny," she said. "I fell on a lot of nice soft dog. I want to do that again." She climbed back onto the seat and pushed herself off on purpose.

"Don't," said Sprout. "He's a dog, not a rug."

"He looks like a rug," said Tilly.

"What will you do with him?" Raymond asked. "Take him to the police?"

Sprout stared straight ahead. "I don't know," he said. "We'll have to think."

"We'll have to think," repeated Tilly solemnly, and landed on the dog again.

"Stop it," shouted Sprout. "It's cruel!" He suddenly felt very protective about the dog, who sat there so big and so lost, and so kindly letting itself be landed on. It had given him a lot of trouble, but that wasn't its fault.

"I wonder if they're still carol-singing," wondered Raymond. "We might see them."

The taxi slowly turned a corner. "Nearly there," called out Bert. "You all right?"

"We're still here," answered Sprout. He couldn't truthfully say that anything was all right; and the nearer they came to home, the more mixed his feelings were. Raymond, for once, was much calmer; but then, his mother merely thought he was out carol-singing on the minister's back.

"That minister ought to be worried," said Raymond almost smugly, "losing two of us."

"I imagine he'll just think 'Good, more mince pie,'" muttered Sprout. He knew this was a nasty thought, but at the moment he didn't feel nice about anything.

"Hey," called Bert suddenly. "Police car!"

Sprout looked out of the back window and saw a car with a light on top, catching up on them.

"It can't be after me," said Bert. "I haven't done more than twenty since we started."

"Maybe they're after a burglar," offered Sprout.

"Or somebody's been run over," suggested Raymond.

"No, they'd be sounding their siren," said Bert. "Probably just a patrol car. Routine stuff. What a way to spend Christmas, eh?"

Sprout was just thinking that it would be a very good way — he had always wanted to ride in a police car — when Bert suddenly jammed on the brakes. This time, Tilly fell onto the dog without meaning to.

"They're flagging me down," remarked Bert with surprise. "What's the idea? I wasn't speeding—you all can witness that. Never went over the white line. Stopped at the red light . . ." He had pulled the taxi to a halt; the police car had drawn up just in front. Bert kept the engine on and stayed in his seat; his ears looked like question marks.

Two policemen got out of the car, one from each side.

"Whatever it is, I'm innocent," said Bert. "Or have you lost your way?" He grinned at the first policeman, who grinned back.

"All right, Bert, we recognized your old boneshaker. Only stopped to ask if by any chance you'd seen . . . Hey! Who've you got in there?" The policeman's face appeared at the window. The second policeman came up behind him.

"Well, I'm blessed," he said. "It's them!" He opened the door, and Tilly immediately fell out.

Sprout stared at the policeman who was turning her right side up.

"I know you," he said. "You're Officer Chad."

"Tell the others, quickly!" Officer Chad said to the second policeman.

But before anyone had time to tell anyone anything, the doors of the police car burst open, and out came Sprout's mother, Raymond's mother, the minister, and Albina Chad.

"Quite a crowd," remarked Bert, switching off his engine.

Sprout's mother rushed toward them as Raymond's mother exclaimed, "At last!" and burst into tears; the minister started talking loudly; and Albina squealed out, "Look, they've got him!"

Over the general hubbub, Officer Chad said firmly: "Come along, we can't talk here. Better get in the cars again, go home, and sort it out."

"I know what," said Sprout, "let's change cars. Come on." And before they could stop him, he had pushed the big dog into the police car, where it seemed quite content to go.

"Me too!" squeaked Tilly, and fell in on top of it.

"Can I?" Raymond asked his mother, but she was too upset to answer.

"Yes, come on," said Sprout. "Bert'll take the others." He settled comfortably into the back seat. A ride in a police car! It was his first happy moment for hours.

"Well, I'm blessed," said Officer Chad again. "Sorry, sir," he grinned at the minister, "somebody seemes to have organized things, hasn't he?"

"Never mind," said the minister. "Thank heavens we've — "

"But the dog? How did he get that dog?" Sprout's mother sounded very much bewildered.

"It's him," nodded Albina.

"We'll go into that later," said Officer Chad. "You people had better get into the taxi; it's cold standing out here."

"Oh, well, it all makes a change," said Bert. "Still Penzance Gardens, is it?"

"Yes," said the policeman. "You'd better follow me. I'll go on in front."

"Make sure you don't do over thirty!" Bert winked. "We don't want to lose you!"

"I'll take that mistletoe off your ear!" beamed Officer Chad, trotting back to his own car.

So that was how they all went home. Sprout had hardly exchanged a word with his mother yet; but he was determined to enjoy the drive while it lasted and not to think of the fuss that was ahead.

"This dog seems to like this car," he said. The dog had lain down on the floor, just as if it was at home by the fire.

"He knows it," said Officer Chad rather grimly.

6

When they got to Sprout's house, the door was opened by Mrs. Chad. Sprout was surprised to see her there at that time of day — but not so surprised as she was to see all of them; especially the dog.

"You've got him!" she said, just as Albina had. "Wherever did you find them all — but where's Albina?" she added shrilly. "Don't tell me you've gone and lost *her*!"

"Take it easy," said her husband. He propelled Raymond and Tilly and Sprout and the dog into the house. "She's all right. She's coming up behind, in the tin lizzie." He jerked his head toward the road, where Bert's taxi was just arriving.

"For goodness sake, whatever gave you that?" Mrs. Chad stared at Tilly's bump. "Come along into the warm; you might have caught your death. I've got the kettle on." She bustled them all into the kitchen.

"I fell downstairs and had mince pie," said Tilly.

"Here's your smock," said Sprout. Mrs. Chad took it, looking amazed. "And your shoes," added Sprout. "They're wet, but so were my boots."

"Whatever next!" Mrs. Chad gasped. "I thought you were going carol-singing, not to a costume party!"

"We were," said Sprout glumly. He had heard his mother's voice in the hall. Now for the fuss.

Suddenly the kitchen seemed to be full of people, all talking at once.

"Thank goodness, thank goodness," the minister kept saying loudly.

"I should never have let you go," moaned Raymond's mother.

"Tilly, are you all right? Sprout, what d'you mean by it? The minister's been looking for ages. I had to call the police. I don't know what I'd have done without Officer Chad . . ." Sprout's mother was red with relief and agitation.

"I didn't mean to let him out," piped Albina.

Then the minister said he had searched and searched and had come to Sprout's house as a last resort. It was lucky he had arrived there at the same time as Officer Chad . . .

Who said he had had a radio message in his patrol car, and when he heard the address of the missing children, he thought he might as well call there to have a word with Sprout's mother . . .

Who said she would never have gone in the police car if it hadn't been for the arrival of Mrs. Chad . . .

Who swore she would have stayed there all night if need be, and perhaps that dog was a blessing in disguise. But what about Tilly's bump?

"I've got a sore head, and Raymond's got a sore ankle," said Tilly.

"It's lucky Bert's aunt knew a taxi," said Raymond.

"Well, will that be all, then?" said Bert in the background.

The only ones who didn't say anything at all were Sprout and the dog. Sprout was wondering whose dog it was and why Mrs. Chad and Albina had come out on such a snowy night. A thought struck him.

"Did you come to bring us a Christmas present?" he asked Mrs. Chad.

"Sprout!" said his mother; but before she had time to scold him, the telephone rang. "That may be your father," she said. "He's working late tonight. Goodness knows what he'll say when he hears all this . . ."

"I'll be going, then," said Bert. "So long, all."

"You might as well stay for a hot cup of tea," said Mrs. Chad. "Seeing you're one of the rescue party." She had made the tea, and was pouring it into mugs on the kitchen table.

Bert was just taking his when Sprout's mother came back. "It's a Mrs. Wagstaff," she frowned. "Does anybody — "

"Aunt May!" said Bert. He dropped his mug like a hot brick and rushed into the hall.

"Hello, Aunt," they heard him saying. "It's Bert. Yes, they're all right. Everything's under control. I'm just having a — oh. All right, then. O.K. Yes, I'll be there."

He came back into the kitchen looking rather sheepish. "That was my Aunt," he said. "Wanting to know whether the kids were back. Especially the little girl. I'm afraid I'll have to leave that, though" — he looked regretfully at the mug — "she wants me to give

her a lift home. Well, so long. Merry Christmas. All's well that ends well, eh? Which it won't be if I keep Aunt May waiting on the doorstep!" He grinned ruefully. Then he gave Tilly the mistletoe from behind his ear, patted the dog, ruffled Sprout's tuft, and hurried out.

"I like Bert," announced Tilly.

"I didn't like his aunt much," Raymond said. "Still, I suppose it was nice of her to make sure we got back."

"Ping-Pong's a silly name," said Sprout. It was the

first thing he had said, and it was all he really wanted to say; but suddenly they all turned on him and demanded an explanation. Not of the name, but of the whole evening. He sighed. He hated explaining things; but he did his best. He was just telling about how he found the dog and thought it was Auntie's lost one, when Mrs. Chad interrupted.

"Just think, and there were we, looking for him all over! It's a wonder you could hold him, though."

"Tilly couldn't," said Sprout. "That's why — hey," he broke off, "is he your dog?"

"No, he's not," said Officer Chad flatly. "He's a visitor."

"A visitor!" Sprout suddenly saw the light. Hadn't Albina said they were having a visitor for Christmas?

"That thing ours? Over my dead body!" Mrs. Chad put in. "Not that I dislike him, but — "

"I do," said Albina. "Too big."

"He's not!" said Sprout hotly. "He's just a proper dog." Not like Ping-Pong, he nearly added. Secretly, he didn't think she was a proper dog at all.

"A proper nuisance," said Mrs. Chad. "Getting out; taking up the fireplace; eating us out of house and home. I doubt if we'll get any Christmas dinner, not with him around."

"Come off it, don't exaggerate," said Officer Chad. "He hasn't had anything today, except for my steak — "

"And my licorice," said Albina.

"And all that bread I put out for the birds," said Mrs. Chad.

"And a chop," said Sprout.

"My Daddy's dinner. He even ate the bone," squeaked Tilly.

Sprout's mother went and looked in the pantry. The dog followed her.

"He wants the other one," said Sprout.

"But who on earth," his mother began, "gave him . . ."

"Well, if you'll excuse me," the minister broke in cheerfully, "I think I'd better be getting along." He felt that there were family fights ahead, which were none of his business. "I told the rest of the choir to assemble for the mince pies if they didn't find the wanderers; I expect they're eating now. I'll just go along and tell them all's well."

"We have to go, too," said Raymond's mother. "I only hope he hasn't done his ankle any harm. I should never have allowed him to go . . ."

"I'm glad I did," said Raymond. "Snow's good for tracking."

"Oh dear, I don't know if you should walk home; we should have asked that young man with the taxi . . ."

"Oh pooh," said Raymond under his breath. And then, quite loudly, "I'm all right and it was the best evening I've had for a long time." And he hobbled out, refusing to take his mother's arm. Sprout thought again that Raymond had perked up a lot since he had been run over.

"We'd better be leaving, too," said Officer Chad. "I imagine you'll be wanting to get them to bed."

Sprout's mother was bathing Tilly's bump; Albina watched, impressed.

"Does it hurt?" she asked.

"Yes," said Tilly proudly; but Sprout knew that if it had, she would have been howling. He also knew that as soon as the Chads left, his mother would turn her attention to him. He wasn't looking forward to it.

"What about the dog?" asked Mrs. Chad.

"Well, *what about* him?" Officer Chad repeated with a rather glazed look. "A promise is a promise. We'll have to take him home, that's all."

"And there's our Christmas ruined," cried Mrs. Chad.

"I don't like him. He's too big," wailed Albina. She backed away from the dog.

"There! *She* can't stand him, and *I* say he's a nuisance, and as for him, all he wants is out. But no, we've got to have him for Christmas," she finished bitterly.

"Why?" asked Sprout. "Whose is he?"

"He belongs to an old gentleman," said Officer Chad. "Or did. But the old man's too old to look after him — "

"I'm not surprised," sniffed Mrs. Chad.

"— What with his rheumatism, and the dog being an active dog — "

"Active! He's a whirlpool!"

"Whirlwind, you mean," said Officer Chad patiently. "Which again is a slight exaggeration. He's just got a lot of energy. So anyway," he told Sprout, "the old gentleman happening to know me as the local police-man, asked me if I'd take the dog off his hands until we could find a good home. I didn't like to refuse, especially since it's Christmas time." Mrs. Chad snorted. "You'd have done the same," the policeman protested. "The old man was getting really worried. Well, he practically begged me. Said he couldn't give it enough exercise, couldn't get out to buy it meat — "

"It's had exercise tonight," said Sprout. "And meat."

"Yes, well, perhaps he'll settle down for a day or two — "

"Not him!" said Mrs. Chad. "And Albina is scared stiff."

"I'm sorry," sighed the policeman, "but what can I do? I couldn't know he'd turn out to be such a handful."

"He's not," said Sprout. "He's just strong. And likes going for walks. And eating. And he *did* settle down," he added, "by Auntie May's stove, with Ping-Pong. He put his chin on his paws." Sprout's tuft seemed actually to bristle in defense of the dog.

"And he had a piece of mince pie," said Tilly. "Like me. He's a nice dog."

"I'm not saying he's *not* nice," sighed Officer Chad. "It's just that — "

"He's too big," whimpered Albina again. "I don't want him home for Christmas."

"Well, I do," said Sprout very firmly.

"So do I!" squeaked Tilly.

"There you are, so does she!" Sprout announced to his mother. For once he was really pleased with Tilly for copying him.

"Don't be silly," their mother began, "you heard Officer Chad say — "

"A good home," said Sprout. "Well, this *is* one!" He beamed so triumphantly at his mother that she found it hard not to beam back.

"I'm glad you think so," she smiled, "but — "

"We have a lot of food," he told the policeman, "and go for a lot of walks. And I like elephants, and they're much bigger than him." He pointed to the dog, who was still standing near the pantry door.

"Can we give him that other chop and keep him?" Sprout asked. "Please?" he added, because he saw that his mother was going to object.

"It would be a godsend if you did," said Mrs. Chad. "Maybe we'd get some Christmas dinner after all."

"Now hold on," said Officer Chad. "I can't just go and give the dog away without permission. I'd have to ask the old gentleman first. Maybe if we take the dog home now, and then after Christmas — "

"Oh no, Dad!" wailed Albina. "Not after Christmas!"

"No," said Sprout. "Now."

"Look here" — his mother was thoroughly flustered — "I'm not having you going anywhere or doing anything else tonight, and that's that. You've had quite enough excitement for one evening."

"I know!" said Sprout. "Call him up!" He radiated enthusiasm for this brilliant idea. After all, Auntie May had rung up his house twice, and his mother had called the police. He realized for the first time what a useful thing the telephone was. Generally his mother had boring calls with friends or shops, and his father still more boring ones to the office; but now at last the phone might do something really good. He looked at the dog, and its black beads looked back at him. He was sure it agreed.

A few moments later, Officer Chad found himself in the hall, dialing a number. Sprout's mother found herself being given another cup of tea by Mrs. Chad, who kept saying, "Of course he's a lovely dog really, it's a shame we couldn't keep him, only . . ." Sprout's mother had great misgivings about that "only"; but Tilly had just tried to climb onto the dog's back, and had fallen off, so there was hardly time to argue or discuss . . .

Sprout never did leave time for people to do these things, anyway. He had followed the officer to the phone and stood squarely there listening to the beginning of the conversation.

". . . Yes, well the thing is," Officer Chad was saying, "it isn't that I've got anything personal against the dog, Mr. Macgready, not at all, only there's a young gentleman here who . . . Well as a matter of fact he found him. In the road. No, of course he shouldn't, but it seems my little girl inadvertently opened the back door, and . . ."

"Can I speak to him?" asked Sprout.

"Eh? What? Just a moment. Ssh!" he hissed at Sprout. "He's a bit upset the dog got out. I'm trying to explain . . . Yes, Mr. Macgready, I'm still here."

"So am I," said Sprout.

"Well, sir, there appears to be some idea that the finder might be willing to keep the dog, and as we've had a certain amount of difficulty with the animal, I wondered — "

"Let me ask him," said Sprout. "I'm the one who found it."

"Pipe down," said Officer Chad out of the corner of his mouth. "— No, sir, sorry, I didn't mean you, sir. It's the finder. He's here with me. As I was saying, I wondered if you'd consider — "

"Hello!" shouted Sprout into the telephone. He could wait no longer; Officer Chad was altogether too wordy for his liking. He had climbed up onto the stool by the telephone, so that his tuft was on a level with the policeman's head.

"Hello!" he shouted again.

"Who's that?" asked a startled, crusty old voice.

"Sprout," said Sprout.

"I'm sorry, sir," began Officer Chad. "It's the young gentleman who — "

"I found your dog, and then I lost him again, and then I tracked him with a chop. Can I keep him?"

There was a silence at the other end. Then the voice, which had a Scotch accent, said, "Could you repeat that, please?"

So Sprout repeated it, and added, "This is a good home. And there's still another chop left."

"Where's the dog now?" asked the voice.

"In the kitchen," said Sprout. "He can have an old blanket in the corner. He can even have my coat!" he shouted anxiously. "And that's new!"

The voice asked to speak to Officer Chad again.

"All right," said Sprout. "But they don't want him, and I do. And so does Tilly." He gave Officer Chad the phone.

When they both went back to the kitchen, the officer was looking rather happier than before, but Sprout was absolutely radiant. His face was pink, his eyes were like bright blue buttons, and his hair stood up as if it was ready to jump off the top of his head.

"He says yes!" he announced.

"Oh dear . . ." murmured his mother.

"What a blessing!" exclaimed Mrs. Chad. "Now we can breathe again!"

"We don't have to have him for Christmas, then?" said Albina; she actually broke into a scraggy little grin.

"But who's going to look after it?" said Sprout's mother desperately.

"I am," said Sprout.

"Me, too," added Tilly.

"I reckon this deserves another cup of tea," said Mrs. Chad, beaming. "He's a lovely-*natured* dog," she assured Sprout's mother. "It's only that Albina couldn't seem to take to him. *She* has, though," she added. "Just look at that!" She pointed to Tilly, who was lying on the floor letting the dog lick her bump.

Sprout grinned approvingly. "Hey," he said, "have we got any mince pies? I missed them all."

"D'you mean to say you've actually got your appetite back?" said his mother.

In the next ten minutes, Sprout showed that he had.

"Sprout's stuffing again," said Tilly.

"I'm like that dog," said Sprout through the crumbs of his fifth piece of pie.

In fact, they did look slightly alike, except that the dog's hair fell down, whereas Sprout's stuck up. But they were both beady-eyed and solid.

"There you are," said Mrs. Chad as she left. "That dog'll be a good tonic for him. Just what he needs."

"Yes," nodded Sprout with his mouth full.

Later that evening, the minister called to ask if Sprout was all right, and to say he was sorry both boys had missed the coffee and mince pies.

"Don't worry," said Sprout's mother. She was covered with flour; she had been frantically rolling out a new pie.

"But tell him we'll still be very glad to see him in the choir tomorrow morning," said the minister, "if he wants to trot along."

"Trot where?" asked Sprout suspiciously. He had heard this over the banister.

"To church," his mother said. Then she thanked the minister and told him she was sure Sprout would come.

"But I was going to take him for a walk!" exploded Sprout. "His Christmas walk. I told him!"

"Told who what?" His mother wiped some flour off the telephone with her apron; she had only just gotten Tilly to bed and felt very much flustered and run off her feet. Then she saw two huge woolly paws sticking through the banisters on the landing above.

"Sprout!" she said. "You are *not* to take that dog upstairs! I will not have him in the bedrooms!"

"He's not," said Sprout.

"Bring him down, at once. I'm not at all sure that I want him anywhere, for that matter. You heard Mrs. Chad say what a nuisance he was."

"She said he was just what I need," said Sprout. He came downstairs in his pajamas, with bare feet, holding the dog's collar.

"It's all very well . . ." his mother began.

"He's made me hungry again," said Sprout firmly. "All right, I *will* go to church, if you'll let me keep him. I'll be in the choir. I'll wear one of those things. Then I'll take him for a walk afterward."

Sprout's mother looked at him. Certainly he seemed to be pinker and squarer and more his old self already. She looked at the dog. Its black beads looked back; its stumpy tail wagged; it began to lick the flour off her hand.

Sprout knew he had won.

"By the way," he said, "I don't know what he was called before, but now he's called Chops. Tilly and I decided."

On Christmas morning, the minister himself helped to hitch Sprout into a huge black cassock and to safety-pin him into an enormous white surplice with a pie-frill around the neck. He didn't mind at all. He was the pinkest and happiest person in the choir.

"And if you ever want to go out," he told his mother over his third helping of turkey at dinner, "I know a dogsitter."

Chops lay on the floor by Sprout's chair and grunted.

"Anyway, he won't need a sitter," added Sprout. "He's got me."